# BUMPER to BUMPER

*Also by Annie Owen*

Annie's abc
Annie's one to ten

# BUMPER to BUMPER

pop!

chugga

ding-a-ling    fssss    fsssssss1

taoooot!

## Annie Owen

Alfred A. Knopf ⟍ New York

For Rufus, with love

THIS IS A BORZOI BOOK PUBLISHED BY ALFRED A. KNOPF, INC.

Copyright © 1990 by Annie Owen
All rights reserved under International and Pan-American Copyright Conventions.
Published in the United States by Alfred A. Knopf, Inc., New York. Distributed
by Random House, Inc., New York. Originally published in Great Britain as
*Traffic Jam* by Orchard Books, London, in 1990.

ISBN: 0-679-81448-5 (trade)    ISBN: 0-679-91448-X (lib. bdg.)
Library of Congress Catalog Card Number: 90-61964
First American Edition, 1991
Manufactured in Belgium
1  2  3  4  5  6  7  8  9  10

Load the car, climb inside. We're on our way to a birthday party! Step on the gas, we don't want to be late. Let's join the traffic on Highway 8.

Ding-a-ling! Ding-a-ling! Vrooom! That red sports car is going too fast. Squeak! A lady on a bicycle is going too slow.

What noise the traffic makes! So many cars, so many trucks. We hope we don't have long to wait, bumper to bumper…on Highway 8.

Weeoo! Weeoo! What's that sound? Fire engines are speeding to a fire. The police car clears the lane. Everyone has to get out of the way quickly.

Move to the side! A fire can't wait. Let the fire
fighters through...on Highway 8.

Clank! Clank! A car pulling a trailer is having engine trouble. Rumble! Rumble! A red flatbed truck is rolling by.

Look! There's a giraffe right in back of us. And that car with a flat tire might make other drivers wait, bumper to bumper...on Highway 8.

Slooosh, slooosh. The road-cleaning truck is cleaning the road. It is so slow. An auto transport is stuck behind it.

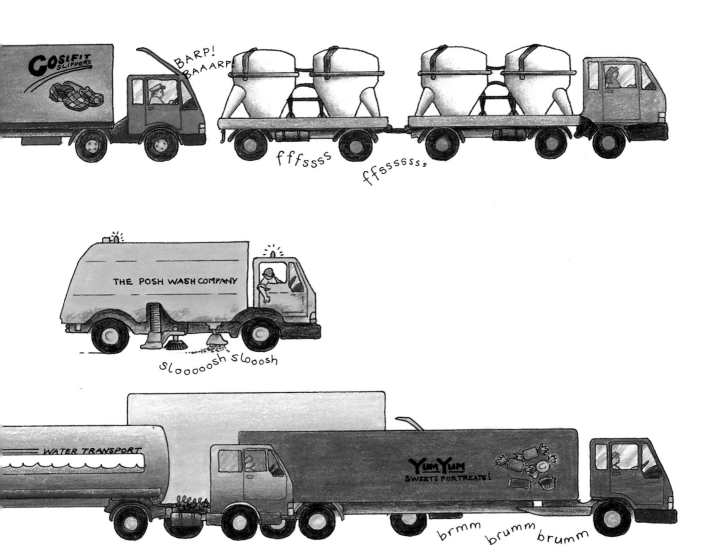

See all the tankers, semi-trucks, and tractor-trailers?
All kinds of trucks full of all kinds of freight! And
they're bumper to bumper...on Highway 8.

Screech! A white sports car comes to a stop.
There's been an accident. No one is hurt, but three
cars must be towed away.

Now everybody is held up in this traffic jam: cars,
trucks, vans. We hope we don't miss our party
date, waiting bumper to bumper…on Highway 8.

Beep! Beep! What's holding up traffic now?
Sheep! Everyone has to stop—the logging truck,
the sports car, the van.

Hey, there's a dog chasing those sheep! This view from our window is really great, waiting bumper to bumper...on Highway 8.

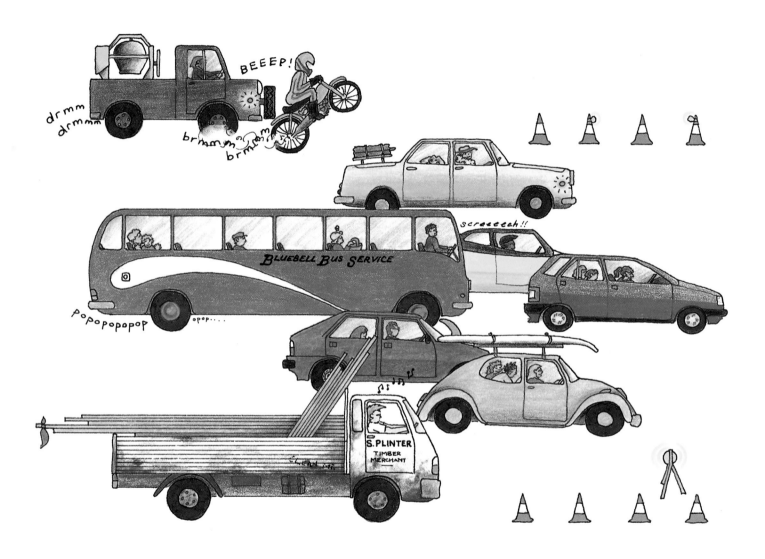

Slow down! Road construction ahead. Phut, phut goes the yellow steamroller. Beep, beep goes the big orange front-end loader. Dugga-dugga goes the little dump truck.

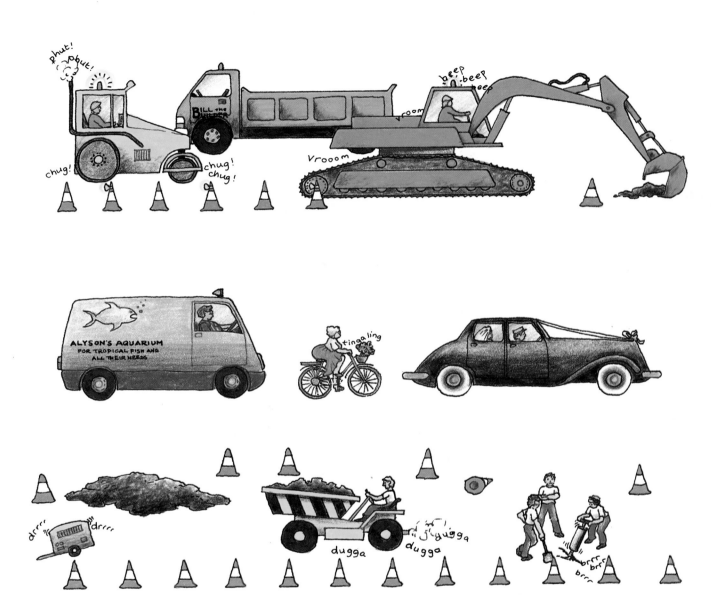

All traffic squeezes into the middle lane. We just hope we're not too late, still waiting and waiting... on Highway 8.

Ting-a-ling! It's a bicycle race! How many bikes are rolling along? How many bikes have something wrong?

Uh-oh. An ambulance is trying to come through.
Move out of the way! We'll all have to wait, as the
ambulance goes down...Highway 8.

Oompah-pah! Oompah-pah! Here's a parade. A
truck is carrying three clowns with orange balloons.

A majorette twirling a baton leads the way. We're almost there. Isn't it great? We're about to get off...
Highway 8!

At last! We're here. Pull over…stop the car. It's time to get out. We hope we're not late. Hello, birthday girl! Good-bye…Highway 8!